THE ZEEBS

To th Carson Crew
Have fun
reading everyday!

To Alex— walk your own path
and happiness will join you.

by Tim Janz
Illustrated by
Jennifer Taylor

Tim Janz

Book design by Jennifer Taylor

Note for Librarians: A cataloguing record for this book is available from Library and Archives
Canada at www.collectionscanada.ca/amicus/index-e.html
ISBN 1-4120-5625-X

*Printed in Victoria, BC, Canada. Printed on paper with minimum 30% recycled fibre. Trafford's print shop
runs on "green energy" from solar, wind and other environmentally-friendly power sources.*

Offices in Canada, USA, Ireland and UK
This book was published *on-demand* in cooperation with Trafford Publishing. On-demand
publishing is a unique process and service of making a book available for retail sale to the
public taking advantage of on-demand manufacturing and Internet marketing. On-demand
publishing includes promotions, retail sales, manufacturing, order fulfilment, accounting and
collecting royalties on behalf of the author.

Book sales for North America and international:
Trafford Publishing, 6E–2333 Government St.,
Victoria, BC v8t 4p4 CANADA
phone 250 383 6864 (toll-free 1 888 232 4444)
fax 250 383 6804; email to orders@trafford.com
Book sales in Europe:
Trafford Publishing (UK) Ltd., Enterprise House, Wistaston Road Business Centre,
Wistaston Road, Crewe, Cheshire cw2 7rp UNITED KINGDOM
phone 01270 251 396 (local rate 0845 230 9601)
facsimile 01270 254 983; orders.uk@trafford.com
Order online at:
trafford.com/05-0523

10 9 8 7 6 5 4 3 2

People from all over the world travel thousands of miles to visit the beautiful continent of Africa. These people travel here, hoping to see many strange and exotic animals. Can you imagine how exciting it would be to feel the earth shake under your feet as a herd of elephants strolled by? Or to watch a pride of lions and listen to them roar while they lounged in the long grass? And what fun to see a long necked giraffe picking leaves off the tallest branches of a tree.

And although it is a great thrill to see any of these sights, it is unfortunate that these people will never see the most amazing animal of them all! As the people gaze in awe at the large creatures of Africa, they miss seeing something right under their feet! Would you believe there is a tiny zebra that could fit in the palm of your hand? Yes, this is true. I know where to find these little zebras. Would you like to see? Then come with me to a magical place, hidden on the plains of Africa.

Zoe Zeeb was the prettiest of all the mini zebras. Her fur had magnificent black and white stripes that she kept brushed and cleaned. Her long black mane appeared to be made of velvet as it flowed from the top of her head and down her neck. Zoe's trademark was a bright coloured ribbon tied in her mane. Her right ear seemed to flop to the side slightly, and you couldn't miss Zoe's brilliant smile, which she showed a great deal since she was almost always very happy.

"Oh Zackery, you know you can never keep up with the other zebras," said Zoe to her brother, Zackery Zeeb. "Why must you always try?" she asked.

"With these new running shoes Zoe, I'll be as fast as a cheetah. No one will be able to catch me. You are looking at the new leader of the pack!" exclaimed Zack.

Zackery was the kind of mini zebra that everyone liked. He had a mischievous twinkle in his eyes and a smile that seemed to take up his entire face. Unlike Zoe, Zack's mane was usually somewhat scruffy. This was due to Zack's love of adventure, which meant his fur was also dusty and dirty more often than not. Zack's striped tail could wag so fast it actually made a humming noise.

"That's leader of the herd," corrected Zoe. "It can be very dangerous to run with the big animals. I'm afraid you'll be hurt."

"No worries, sis. I can take care of myself. The big zebra stampede should be starting any minute," Zack said excitedly.

Every afternoon on the plains, the big zebras would organize a stampede. Forming together in a large group, they would run as fast as they could across the land. None of the other animals understood why the zebras did this, but it made the zebras happy, so no one seemed to mind.

Soon after Zoe ran home, Zack could hear the distant pounding of hooves and a huge gray cloud of dust filled the horizon. Zack took his mark, and waited for the wild herd of stampeding zebras to run by. His heart was pounding as the leaders of the herd were nearly upon him. Then like a shot, Zack jumped to the front of the line. As he zigged and zagged across the grassy plain, the zebras zigged and zagged with him. The air was clean at the front, and Zack loved the feel of the wind whistling through his mane. The long grass seemed to part before him in honour of his coming. On and on he went, giggling as he ran. He really was the leader of the herd!

But suddenly Zack was running in mid-air! Sploosh! The tiny zebra landed right in a pond of water. The other zebras ran quickly past, hardly noticing their "leader" had vanished. Zack was disheartened as he watched the last of the herd disappear.

"**O**h wazzlepop! I'll never catch them now. Hey, I don't remember this pond being here before," Zack exclaimed aloud.

"**T**hat's because it's not a pond you silly zebra," said Turtle who sat gazing at Zack in the water.

"**H**i Turt! Where did you come from?" asked Zack.

"**I** was just hiding in my shell until the stampede passed. I wish I knew why you zebras insist on running around like that," said Turtle.

"**J**ust got to do it Turt. Just got to do it. Hee hee!" giggled Zack.
"Hey what did you mean this isn't a pond?"

"It is a footprint from that bull elephant, Big Bomba. He is so heavy he made a hole in the ground with his foot, and yesterday it filled with rain," answered Turtle.

"Do you mean Big Bomba made this pond? Wow! He is huge!" Zack cried excitedly.

"Yes my friend, and you should run along since he may be returning soon. I'm heading for the river myself if you would like to join me," offered Turtle.

"No thank you, Turt. I'm going to take a swim since I'm already wet," Zack said as he floated lazily on his back in the cool water. The warm sun felt relaxing as it shone down on his chubby belly.

Meanwhile Zoe was back at home waiting for her adventurous brother to return. Even with her binoculars she couldn't seem to see any sign of Zack after the stampede. She was more than a little worried.

"**O**h, I just can't see him anywhere. Zackery! Zackery Zeeb! Where are you?" she called. "Oh that zebra.

"**W**here could he possibly be?"

If Zoe had known where Zack was, she would have been even more worried.

As Zack floated carelessly in the pool, he felt a sudden chill as the sun disappeared and the water began to shake. A large shadow covered him, and Zack gazed up into the eyes of Big Bomba.

Before Zack had a chance to cry out, Big Bomba had reached down into the pond with his massive gray trunk, and sucked up all the water, including one surprised little zebra!

Poor Big Bomba. He was thirsty and had only wanted a drink. He didn't even see the tiny zebra swimming in the water, and now his trunk was stuffed full. And poor Zack. Struggle as he might, he could not seem to move.

"**H**mmmm. This is a fine pickle I'm in now. "Hey elephant, let me out," Zack called.

There was no reply. "Hmmmm...," thought Zack.
"I'll have to think of something else."

As Zack concentrated on how to escape, he began to wag his tail, which was a habit of his whenever he had to think hard. His tail began to tickle Big Bomba's trunk, and the elephant suddenly felt the urge to sneeze.

The harder Zack concentrated, the faster his tail wagged, until Big Bomba could no longer withstand the pressure and he bellowed out a mighty elephant sneeze!

Like a screaming cannon ball, Zack shot out across the plain!

"Weeeeeee! This is cool," Zack squealed. " I'm flying. I'm flying. Uh oh. I'm dropping. I'm dropping!"

As magical as they are, miniature zebras are not meant to fly, so Zack's time at being a bird did not last long. Zack buried his head and gritted his teeth preparing for impact. Boom! He hit the ground with a thud and began rolling over and over on the dusty ground.

"Whoa! That was wild! Hee hee hee. Wait until Zoe hears about this one. It's time I got back home to her. She will be worried. Hmmm.... I wonder where I am now? Hey what was that?"

Zack perked his ears toward the noise and froze in fear as he strained to hear the noise again. The sound moved even closer. There was no mistaking the shrill whistles and chattering.

"Poachers. I have to hide!" exclaimed Zack.

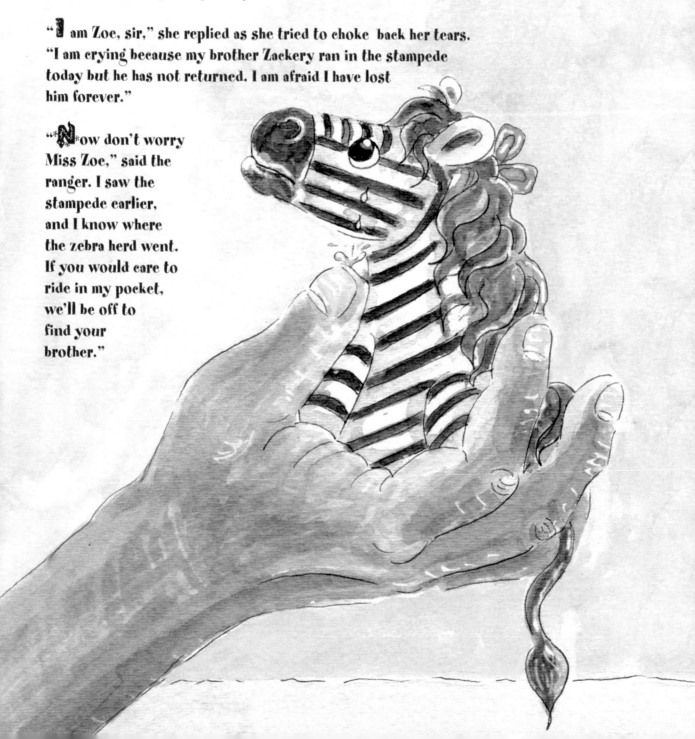

Back at home, Zoe had just about given up hope. She was so worried about Zack, she hadn't noticed there was someone standing over her. Zoe was startled as she was suddenly scooped up and sitting in the hand of a human! Zoe felt comfort in the man's warm smile, and she instantly knew he meant her no harm.

"My name is Ranger Jayba. I am here to protect you and all of the animals," said the man as he showed Zoe his golden badge. "And what is your name little one, and why do you cry today?" he asked.

"I am Zoe, sir," she replied as she tried to choke back her tears. "I am crying because my brother Zackery ran in the stampede today but he has not returned. I am afraid I have lost him forever."

"Now don't worry Miss Zoe," said the ranger. I saw the stampede earlier, and I know where the zebra herd went. If you would care to ride in my pocket, we'll be off to find your brother."

Zack's ears had not failed him. It was indeed poachers and they were moving ever closer toward him. Poachers were bad men who hunted animals in search of profit. They did this even though it was against the law and the animals here were protected against hunting. Zack was right to be afraid, for a miniature zebra would collect a very large sum of money indeed. If captured, he would never see his sister Zoe again.

Zack ran away from the noise as fast as his tiny legs would carry him. Just when he felt he could run no longer, he spotted a cave hidden amongst some trees on the edge of the jungle. Zack scurried toward the shelter to avoid the evil poachers.

Zack collapsed against the wall of the cave, puffing hard from the run. As he began to catch his breath, he peered around the inside of the cave. Suddenly, he was aware of two large yellow eyes glaring down on him.

"Yikes! Who's there?" cried Zack. "Shhhhh. Be quiet rat! The humans will hear you," rumbled the eyes.

"I am no rat," Zack said indignantly. "I'm Zackery the Zebra. Now who are you?" he asked. Before Zack could react, a huge furry paw reached out of the darkness and snatched him up. As he was pulled in closer, Zack realized he was now face to face with the King of the Jungle, the lion.

Zack knew there was no escape, and he shuddered in fear as the lion's huge mouth opened, showing the largest set of teeth Zack had ever seen. Suddenly, the lion's tongue stretched out, and gave Zack a rough sloppy lick right across his body. "Eeeuuk!" spit Zack.

"Why did you do that lion? If you are going to eat me, just get it over with!"

"Ha, ha, ha," the lion chuckled. I can see that you really are a zebra now that your stripes are showing. I do not wish to eat you. I am hiding from the poachers also. They have been hunting me for days and I am too old and too tired to run any longer. My name is Alexander."

" It is a pleasure to meet you Alexander," Zack said respectfully. Zack and his new found friend could hear voices as the poachers approached the entrance to the cave. The whistles, cries, and constant beating of sticks sent a shiver down Zack's back.

"I'm afraid they know I am here Zack. I will prepare to make my final stand. Quickly, you must hide in the back of the cave so the poachers will not find you," ordered Alexander.

A tear slid down Zack's cheek as he gazed up into the solemn face of Alexander the Lion.

"Do not feel sad little brother. It is every lion's dream to die honourably in battle. I will be even more proud to know I have protected you," Alexander said earnestly.

"But Alexander, I will make the final charge with you. The two of us can overpower the men and we can escape," proclaimed Zack jumping up and down in excitement.

"You have a brave heart for one so small, Zackery. But this is my battle today. His stern gaze told Zack that the discussion was over. Sadly, with his head down, Zack walked toward the back of the cave.

Alexander admired Zack for his bravery, but he knew that the little zebra did not stand a chance against the men. He would only be an unexpected profit to the poachers.

Alexander turned and flared his giant white teeth in preparation for his charge.

Before Alexander could make a move, the voices of the men suddenly grew silent. As Alexander peered out into the fading sunlight, he could see the poachers running away. Alexander was even more puzzled to see another man approaching the cave from the opposite direction. This man had a strong sense of purpose and it was obvious that the poachers had run away in fear of him. The man smiled as he watched the poachers scramble away.

By now Zack had crept up beside Alexander to see what had happened and he heard a familiar voice calling his name.

"**Z**ackery, Zackery Zeeb, are you in there?" called Zoe.

"Zack, if you are in the cave please come out. I am with Ranger Jayba who is here to take you home. Oh please come out Zack," hollered Zoe.

Well you can imagine how surprised Zoe and Ranger Jayba were, when the magnificent Alexander strolled lazily out of the cave entrance with a tiny zebra riding on his shoulders.

"I see you Zoe. I am here little sister," shouted Zack.

Brother and sister both ran from their friends to hug each other in celebration. As was a zebra tradition, they rubbed noses together and their tails wiggled in excitement.

"**I** am happy for you my friend. I am indebted to you and your sister for my life. Now that I have this chance for freedom, I must go. Farewell Zackery Zeeb," said Alexander the Lion.

"**F**arewell Alexander. Perhaps we will fight together again someday," smiled Zack hopefully.

"**Y**es perhaps," chuckled the lion as he trotted away into the nearby jungle.

Well, it looks like you've had an interesting day Mr. Zack.
I am sure you are tired and would like to go home. I think there is
enough room for one more zebra in my pocket if you would care
for a ride," said the Ranger.

"Oh yes, sir. Even I've had enough excitement for one day. Let's go home, " sighed Zack.

And so it was that Ranger Jayba traveled back up the African plain with two giggling,
miniature zebras guiding him every step of the way. He was sure he had never heard
two animals chatter quite so much. Miss Zoe was certainly making it quite clear to Mr.
Zack that he was not to be running off in a stampede again. Ranger Jayba smiled to
himself thinking that Mr. Zack could probably find lots of other trouble to get into.
He wondered if anyone would believe his story about two tiny zebras called Zack and
Zoe as he shook his head and laughed. "No, probably not so."